Tweenies™

The Magic Lamp

One morning Judy came in with a huge cardboard box.

"What's in your box, Judy?" asked Bella.

"Just some bits and pieces I'm tidying away," said Judy.

"Let's have a look.
I love bits and pieces," said Milo.
The Tweenies looked inside the box.

There were some coloured beads, a big sparkly ring, a golden crown, a long, black cloak and an old, silver teapot.

"Do you remember the pantomime we saw at Christmas about Aladdin? Why don't we act out the story?" said Bella.

"Is there a princess?" asked Fizz.

"Yes," said Bella, "there's Aladdin and his *mum*, the wicked Uncle Abanazar and two genies, too."

"Oh, can I be Avabanana?" said Jake. "I'm feeling wicked today."

So Bella was both genies, Milo was Aladdin, Fizz was the princess and Aladdin's *mum*, Jake was Abanazar and Doodles was the wicked Smutley. Judy told the story.

Once upon a time there was a boy called Aladdin.

"That's *me*!" said Milo.

Aladdin lived with his *mum*, but he was very lazy and never helped out around the house.

"Oh, Aladdin. You're such a lazy boy!" said Fizz. "I wish we were rich and I didn't have to work so hard."

One day, someone dressed in black appeared in the garden.

"Who are you?" asked Aladdin.

"I'm your Uncle Avabanana – I mean Ab-an-ar-zar," said Jake.

"Do you fancy a peanut butter sandwich?" asked Aladdin.

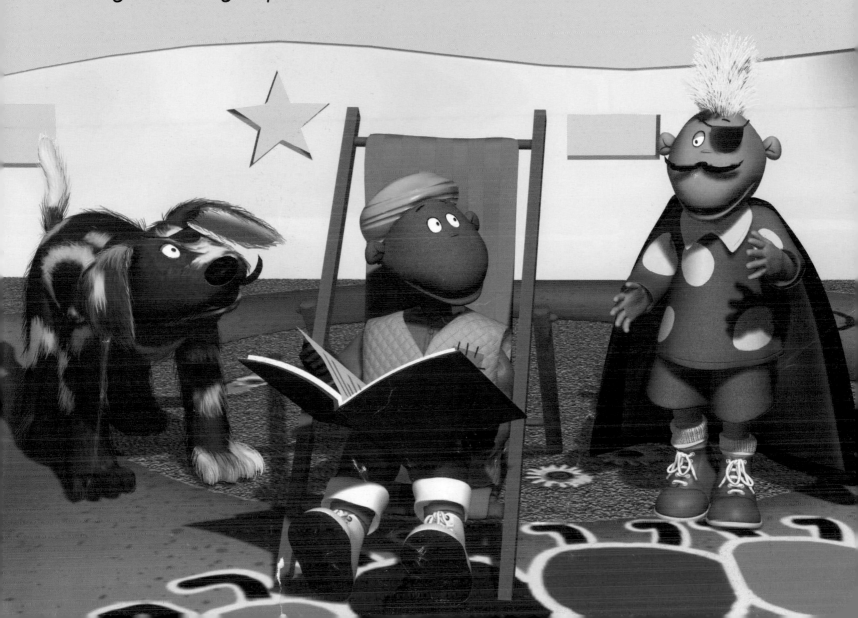

Uncle Abanazar munched greedily on the peanut butter sandwich and then he took Aladdin for a long walk. Finally, they arrived at the entrance to a cave.

Now, Abanazar wouldn't go into the cave because it could destroy bad people. But he knew that there was something inside that would make him rich and powerful.

"Listen, Aladdin, I want you to fetch me an old lamp from inside this cave," he said.

"Looks a bit dark," said Aladdin.
  Abanazar threw Aladdin a big,
sparkly ring.
  "This will protect you, scaredy-pants.
Now, in you go," he said. And he gave
Aladdin a big push.

Once inside the cave, Aladdin could hardly believe his eyes. The walls glittered with bright treasure and there were stacks of jewels and gold coins in every corner.

"Wow! Glitter-ooney!" said Aladdin.

As he walked around, he slipped a few gold coins into his pockets. Then he searched for the lamp.

"Found it!" he called out at last.

"Give it to me!" shouted Abanazar from outside.

"No way! You let me out first," said Aladdin.

"No – I want that lamp!" cried Abanazar, and he tried to climb in. As he did, a huge stone rolled in front of the entrance and, with a scream of rage and a puff of smoke, Abanazar disappeared.

Poor Aladdin was shut in the cave. Suddenly, his fingers rubbed against the ring his uncle had given him and there was a terrific...

WHOOSH!

Someone appeared in front of him.

"I am the Genie of the Ring.
What is your wish, oh master?"
said Bella.

"Can I wish for
anything I like?" asked Aladdin.
"Anything – just make it quick. It's cold in
this cave!" the Genie replied.
"OK. I wish I was back home," said Aladdin.
The Genie clapped her hands.

Aladdin's mum was pleased to see him and while the Genie organised a splendid feast, Aladdin told her everything that had happened.

"But why did Abanazar want that old lamp?" asked Mum.
"I don't know," said Aladdin, as he polished it with his sleeve.

Suddenly, there was a terrific...

WHOOSH!

"I am the Genie of the Lamp this time!"
said Bella. "What is your wish, oh master?"
"More wishes!" said Aladdin. "Wish-a-rooney!"

Aladdin wished to become a very rich man, marry a beautiful princess and live in a palace. In no time at all his wishes were granted.

"Oh, Aladdin!" said Fizz. "Aren't you going to kiss your bride?"
"Yuck! No way!" said Milo. "That's not in the story!"

Judy went on quickly.

Anyway, one day, when Aladdin was out, the princess heard someone shouting outside the palace gates, "New lamps for old! New lamps for old."

The princess decided to swap Aladdin's old lamp for a nice new one.

Little did she know the lampseller was really Aladdin's wicked Uncle Abanazar. He quickly snatched Aladdin's old lamp!

"Ha ha ha ha haaa!" said Abanazar.

"You silly princess. Now I have you in my power!"

He rubbed the lamp and the Genie appeared.

WHOOSH!

"I am the Genie of the Lamp! What is your wish, oh master?" said Bella.

"Take this princess to my house. That'll show Aladdin who's boss," ordered Abanazar. The Genie clapped her hands.

When Aladdin found out that his wife and the lamp had disappeared, he guessed it was the work of Abanazar. He went straight to his uncle's house and rescued his princess. Then he took the lamp from the sleeping Abanazar and rubbed it. The Genie appeared again.

WHOOSH!

"I am the Genie of the Lamp. What is your wish, oh master?" she said.

"Please, Genie, can you take me and the princess home, and send that wicked Abanazar into outer space?" asked Aladdin.

"With pleasure!" said the Genie, and with a puff of blue smoke she did just that.

Aladdin and his princess arrived home in one piece. From then on Aladdin kept his lamp with him at all times and the princess was very careful not to talk to lampsellers in black cloaks.

Aladdin, his princess and his *mum* all lived happily ever after...

...and whenever the night sky was clear they would look up at the stars and wonder what had happened to wicked Uncle Abanazar.

"Well done, everyone!" clapped Judy.

The Tweenies took a bow.

"Can I have my teapot back now?" laughed Max.

THE END